BRICK & STICK

Branching Out

Julie Little loves to write her ideas & stories early in the morning while still in her cozy bed. She began teaching elementary school age children at 22 years old.
Julie collaborated with her son, Marc, who she says is amazingly easy and entertaining to work with.
She lives in Rancho Cucamonga, California.
Say it! It will make you smile.

To: Hooey ♡ JL

Marc is an illustrator and author from Rancho Cucamonga, California. He earned his degree in Multimedia Arts from San Diego State University. He loves to draw, make music, and travel.

To: my thugs on the beach — ML

ISBN 978-1-4951-8554-0

Text & illustrations © 2015 Julie & Marc Little
All rights reserved. Published by Hooster Books

BRICK & STICK

Branching Out

by

Julie & Marc Little

Want to see a

slick

trick?

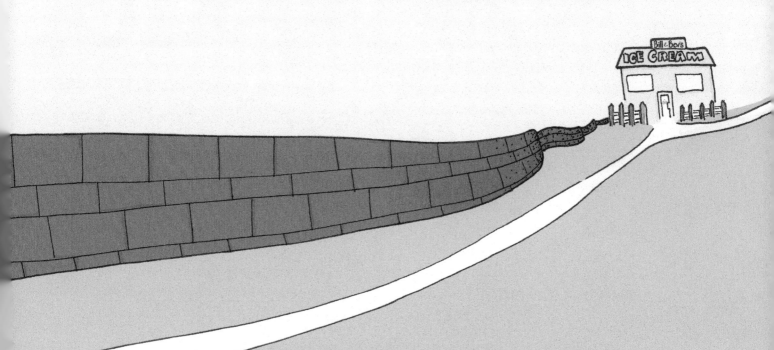

Bill & Boys
ICE CREAM

If you squirm just a bit and give a

big
kick...

we'll be on our way
to see my friend,
Pick!

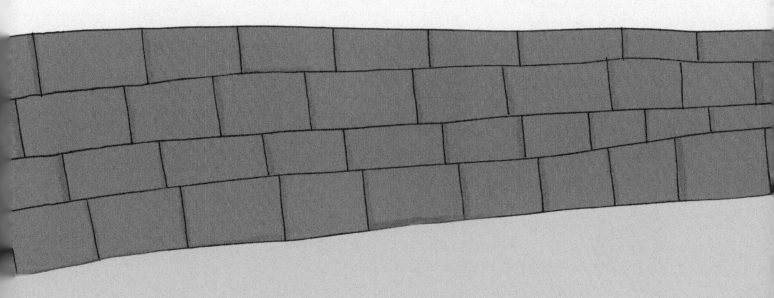

We'll go on an adventure that can't be beat. Today is the day, the world's at our feet!

Brick, Brick, Brick!
See, that's my friend,

Pick!

Hello!

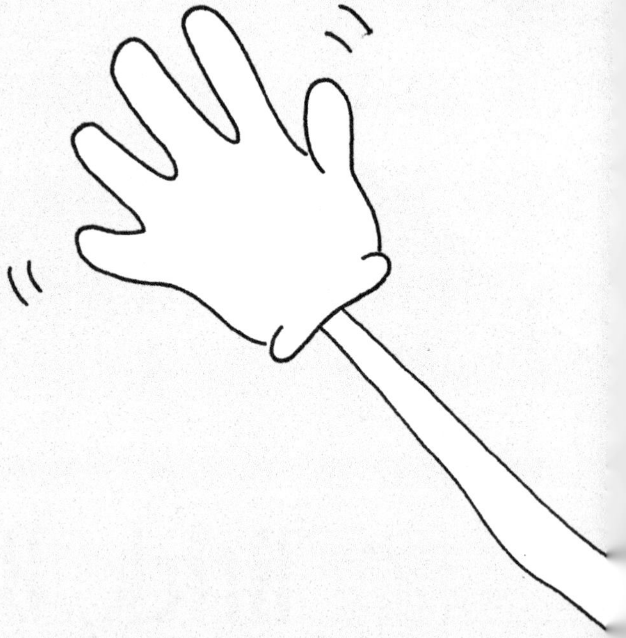

Would you like something sweet?

My home is known for its **magnificent** treats.

They have the best ice cream on a stick.

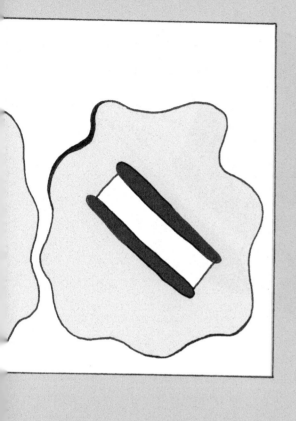

$3.00

Take it slowly and enjoy every lick.

OW!OW!OW!

exclaimed Brick and Stick.

This delicious ice cream is making us

My head really hurts.

What is happening?

GEEZ!

Then out popped **Click** to explain the BRAIN FREEZE

You ignored Pick's advice and ate it too fast.

I promise, my friends,
the pain will not last.

Oh, my friend Click, you are so wise...

But now it is time to say our goodbyes.

Stick, you were right, this adventure was sweet.

Next time we better watch how we eat.

Today has been awesome, we've had a ball, so let's return to your tree and my wall.

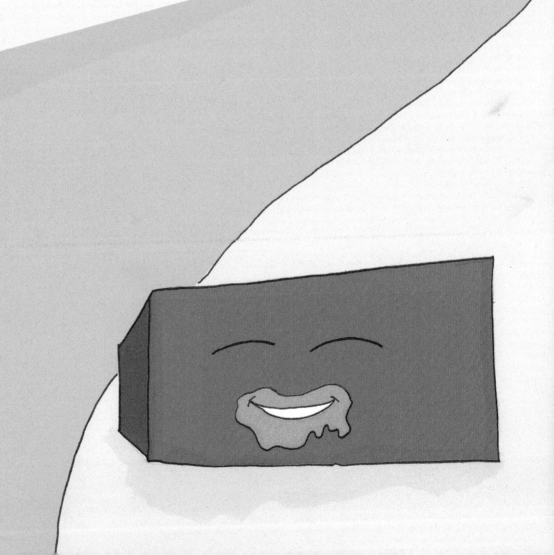

They squirmed just a bit and gave a big kick and returned to their places as Brick & Stick.

CPSIA information can be obtained
at www.ICGtesting.com
Printed in the USA
LVOW05s0532100316

478343LV00018BA/92/P